Fetish Circuit

HONEY POT COLLECTION

Fetish
Circuit

HONEY POT COLLECTION

Ali Whippe

4 Horsemen
Publications, Inc.

Dedication

For all the boys seeking a Mistress

Chapter One

"*So, you like to watch, do you?*" Katie's voice is a low thrum, and Steve doesn't remember her sounding quite so sultry from their days together back in high school.

Hell, did I ever really listen to her back then at all? Probably not.

She certainly didn't have those amazing tits when she was his partner in his science class. Those breasts are largely to blame for this meeting, that short exchange at the reunion leading to the inevitable "We should hang out sometime" to "catch up on each other's lives."

He'd meant he could catch up on some quality time checking out her lovely shape beneath that shirt. He'd been pleasantly surprised when she accepted so readily, but happy at the chance to see her again somewhere beyond the dim lights of the special events room at the Tampa Hyatt.

He likes looking at her.

He likes the way she doesn't blush or look away from him, even though she must know he has spent most of the conversation marveling over the pale curve of cleavage peeking up out of her plain black button down shirt.

Did she even have tits when I sat next to her in high school?

He doesn't remember. Maybe these are fake. Steve has certainly had his hands around several pairs that were in the last ten years. It is a mystery he suddenly wants to solve, and he takes a moment to shift in his seat to accommodate the slight swelling in his pants.

The girl knows how to dress to highlight her attributes. Her jeans are just tight enough to outline an ass in desperate need of smacking, but not tight enough to make him wonder how she is breathing in them. The shirt is blessed with a neckline low enough for him to contemplate that slow tease of cleavage again, though not as low cut as her black dress the night before had been. He tries to stare at her chest only when she isn't looking at him, which turns out to be not very often.

Katie has grown bold over the years, and her gaze rarely leaves his as she speaks, almost daring his eyes to wander. So far, he has only stumbled that way twice, both times returning guiltily to her knowing smirk. The second time, she stopped what she was saying—something about college—grinned a wicked grin he had never expected to see on her face, and put one hand under his chin, tugging it down so her

3

chest filled his entire view while her other hand pulled down her shirt front just far enough for him to glimpse something red and satin and way too lacy to be a regular bra.

Before he even registered what she had done, she had released his chin and her shirt was back in place. For a second, he wondered if he was fantasizing, but then she had followed it up with, "So, you like to watch, do you?"

"Umm.." he stutters, suddenly off balance as he has not been in years. "No!" He pauses, still looking at those demanding eyes. Then he shrugs, giving it up. "Well, yeah," then he adds, "but who doesn't, Katie?"

"It's Katharine now. I haven't been Katie in years," she laughs, a low purr in her throat that is definitely not part of the girl he remembers. "Watching can be entertaining," the woman across from him says, "if the show is worthwhile."

"Show?" he sputters. "Is that what they teach you in that school of yours?" She had told him of her latest grant-funded research at the local university, Abraxus Tasker College.

"No," she replies quite seriously, "those kinds of shows are not academic in any way." She pauses long enough for him to take in what she has said, then adds, "I don't have a degree in voyeurism after all."

"No," he agrees. "Chemistry you said."

Her eyebrow quirks. "You were listening?"

He leans into the table, closer to her. "I always listen."

"But do you obey?"

The question takes him off guard, a little too close to home for comfort. "What?"

"If you listen so well, do you take direction as well? Can you obey?"

This is not a conversation he ever imagined having with Katie—Katharine—the little nerd who had made sure he passed with an A. "What do you mean: obey?"

Her hand darts across the table to land on top of his, pinning it to the smooth wood. He instinctively tries to jerk away, but she barks at him, a short, sharp "No!" that somehow manages to be swallowed by the swells of the conversations around them. His hand freezes in place, and his cock hardens at once. He stares at her.

How does she know? He thinks of the small pile of satin panties hidden under his bathing suits, the secret delight of wearing women's clothes.

She looks at him for a long time, then says, "Don't move" in that same firm voice that makes him swell even more. He sits still, his hand pressed hard against the table top, chest suddenly very full of something he can't explain.

Her lips curl into a wicked grin to match the one he saw earlier, and she says, "You do take direction. Well done." When Steve continues to stare at her, blank faced and stone still, she takes a long sip of her coffee, chuckles, and says, "You are allowed to talk, you know."

"What are you?" Steve breathes, his hand itching to move, to slide closer to her across the table, but he forces it to stay there, a slow tease between desire and action that makes him want to adjust on the cheap plastic seat. He refuses the urge, sitting perfectly still.

Katharine shrugs confidently. "I'm a scientist," she says casually, then adds, "You may move now too."

Steve is amazed to feel his body relaxing, as if her voice has given him permission to release something held too tightly. For a second, his vision swirls as he lets it go, then he shuffles in his chair, hands coming together around the fading heat of his coffee cup. What has she just done to him? "You know what I mean," he says. "That voice!"

"My voice?" she asks innocently, coy now. "What do you mean?"

"You just...were so....demanding," he manages, trying to focus around the sudden hope dawning in his chest. Would she do it to him again?

She shakes her head. "Not me," she says. "You're just in dire need of topping. I bet you'd fold for anybody right now."

"Topping?" he asks, trying to place the word beyond the ice cream context his brain has suddenly decided to play out before him—a vision involving chocolate syrup and Katharine's mouth that forces him to shift again in his chair. "What's that?"

She laughs a little. "You're not serious, are you?" When he doesn't reply, brain caught between his growing erection and the image of

Katharine's mouth, shiny with chocolate, she stops laughing. "Wait, are you serious?"

"About what?"

"About not knowing what topping means."

"Ice cream?" he tries.

She shakes her head at him, eyes quirking. "Have you really lived this long without acting on this?"

Steve is suddenly suspicious of where this conversation is heading. "Acting on what?"

"You're a sub, Steve. You always have been."

"Sub? Like a teacher?"

She takes a deep breath now, as if trying to accept his level of confusion. "No, like a submissive."

"What do you mean?" *She can't really be saying this out loud,* Steve thinks.

She moves slowly, her hand coming across the table and resting gently on top of his. "You've never had anyone top you before, have you?"

"Tup me?" he shakes his head. "I'm not really into that, if that's what you mean..."

"*Top* you," she says, fingers tightening between his, carefully enunciating the word. "Dominate you."

Steve considers pulling his hands back into his lap, but that feeling in his belly is back again, and he restrains himself. Still, something about that isn't right, so he pushes a little against her grip. Her fingers tighten in reflex and suddenly it hurts a little. He imagines her knuckles must be white, straining as she is to keep him inside her grip, but now, now that little glow is right, the promise of something that could grow.

"I've been dominated," he is saying. "My ex always had to be in charge."

"That's not what I mean, and I think you know it," she tells him, hands squeezing for a second even harder, and the bright pain blossoms for an instant and then is gone, replaced by something disturbingly close to ecstasy. The words burn in his mind, and for a second, he doesn't say them, doesn't let them pass his lips, but then she is giving him that look again, that look that will not be denied, and he hears himself speaking so quietly that she probably can't even hear him.

"Please tell me what you mean, Mistress." Apparently, she can hear him because her hands leave his at once, the space where they had been both relieved and missing that sturdy, confident pressure. He wants to flex but refuses, relishing the feeling as needles promise to replace numbness.

"I thought so," she says. "How long has it been for you?"

He doesn't want to tell her, is embarrassed and curious and excited and angry all at once, but the words come out anyway, the need to please her suddenly overwhelming everything else. "Never," he mumbles, then says it again, more loudly, "Never the way I wanted it."

She leans closer to him, relieving him of the burden of speaking out loud, her voice an intimate whisper of control and understanding. "How do you want it?"

"I want it to be real," he admits, astonished to find the words coming so easily, but aware that they have been inside a long time, just waiting for the right person to conjure them forth. "I want to not have to be in control and to have the girl for once really take charge and mean it."

She smiles at him then, a long slow smile that reminds him of how uncomfortable his boxer shorts can get sometimes. "You really want someone to take charge of you, Steven?"

He nods.

"Say it," she says sharply, yet still in that same intimate voice, and he manages to speak.

"Yes, Mistress."

"Well, then," Katharine says, clearly considering. "If you really want to do this, come to my apartment at 9 tomorrow night. Right at 9," she repeats, "and not a minute later, and we'll see what we can do."

"Do..." Steve echoes, then his brain kicks back on, and he asks, timidly, "Will you have sex with me?"

"Maybe," Katharine says in that same almost sweet, not to be argued with voice. "Maybe not."

"Then what will we do?" He is coming out of that sweet feeling now, coming back into his head and his body, a slide that has him both relieved and annoyed at the same time. His cock aches, then starts to subside, that growing

13

sensation in his gut fading as Katharine leans away from him.

"Then," she replies in a normal voice, "you will have the genuine experience you are craving."

Steve is nodding, knowing that this is what he wants but uncertain of how to proceed. "Should...should I bring protection?" he asks, thoughts mingling with a growing excitement in his mind.

Katharine shakes her head. "You're missing the point," she tells him. "This is about more than sex. This is about easing that ache in your belly. That I can certainly do for you."

"You think so?"

"I know so," Katharine says quite confidently, then her voice changes again, and she is serious now, business-like. "We should probably establish some ground rules before we begin..."

Chapter Two

*S*teve stands near the elevator, wrist held out before him, checking his watch. 8:57. Three more minutes. He knows that it will take him less than a minute to walk down the hall, turn the corner, and find himself standing in front of her door. He checked. Her apartment is J, the one all the way at the end, the corner unit. She shares only one wall with K. Steve wonders if she chose the apartment because of that. She could probably make a lot of noise before anyone would hear it, especially if she was in the rooms far away from that one shared wall.

Steve is very aware of neighbors, knowing just how thin some walls can be. He's spent enough nights listening to all of his neighbors going about their lives. Katie—Katharine he reminds himself again—lives in a nicer building by far with much thicker walls. Chemistry must pay well.

He glances at his watch again. 8:58. He takes a moment to check his appearance in the mirror across from the elevators. His hair is fine, short enough to be respectable but not severe. His shirt is simple, button down black hiding the white tank top he wears beneath. He's not sure why he still wears undershirts, but his father always had, and so Steve still does. He appreciates the extra layer during the harsh winters, though the summers always make him contemplate a change. The pants are plain khakis, and he can either dress up or down depending on whether he tucks in his shirt to reveal his belt. He's wearing loafers to complete the look, comfortable but not quite sneakers.

He checks his teeth in the mirror, sniffs his breath, and then peeks at his watch again. 8:59. It's time.

He takes the few steps down the hallway, heart speeding up as he turns the corner, knowing that this time he gets to knock, gets to enter, and then gets to experience...whatever Katharine has in store.

9:00.

He knocks on the door, two hard raps. The door opens inward to reveal a long hallway lined with tasteful paintings. A voice says, "Come in."

Steve steps inside, eyes adjusting to the dimmer light as the door shuts quietly behind him. He turns around to see Katharine flicking the locks with a practiced hand before she turns to lean casually against the locked door. Her gaze doesn't leave his.

Steve tries to keep his eyes on her face as she clearly expects him to do, but he can't help himself from trailing down from that still-so-familiar face, the long unbound dark hair and bright eyes, to the tight blue tank top that reveals a delightful swatch of considerable cleavage, the short black skirt brushing up against the lace tops of black stockings. He thinks she may even have garters holding them up. His eyes leave her thighs and slide down the rest of her to the floor and her feet, one flat on the floor, the other pressed back against the door. His gaze lingers on her feet for a moment. He expected high heels or boots or something, but the idea of those stockinged feet touching his skin, running along him, is enticing.

"You're on time," she says. "Well done." Steve is about to reply, but she cuts him off. "But you do have those wandering eyes," she muses, tongue making a soft tsking sound. "We will have to work on those."

Steve stares at her, now fully focused on her face again, though his mouth has gone dry. "You..."

"Mistress," she corrects him. "When you speak to me, you will call me Mistress."

"Yes, Mistress," Steve says, and his belly tightens along with his cock at the words.

Katharine nods, pleased. "Good," she tells him. "Now go inside, sit down on the kitchen chair, and take off your shoes."

As he turns to obey, Steve wonders at the specificity of her instructions. How long since someone told him exactly what to do like that? He must have still been a child.

The hallway ends in a large open room. A black couch lines the wall to his right, across from the small entertainment center. Between them is a large picture window with a view of the skyline that puts everything else in the apartment to shame. There are sheer white curtains, but they have been pushed to one side to reveal the cityscape outside. Directly before him is an entrance to a galley kitchen, and to the right is a small dinette with four chairs. The chair closest to him has been pulled out from the table and turned around. Steve assumes this is for him and he sits obediently, taking in the door to a small terrace between the table and the TV. He wonders if the outside patio wraps around the kitchen, remembers the doorman and the state of the lobby in this building, and decides that it must. He hopes that they will go outside at some point. The fall weather has definitely arrived with a chill, but not enough to make him shiver. The night air would be even more delicious with naughtiness.

Steve bends down to remove his shoes, glad that he didn't decide to tuck in his shirt because there is the slight chance that it may ride up in the back and reveal the bright pink lace panties he is wearing beneath his pants.

He wants those to be a surprise.

Steve pauses at his socks, wondering if he should take them off as well. She hadn't said to. He places his shoes underneath the chair and sits back, ready for her next command.

Katharine stands at the end of the entry hallway, eyes taking in the sight before her. "I think," she begins in a low voice, "that you are wearing far too many clothes."

Steve looks down at his shirt and pants, then back up at her. He waits, resisting the urge to pull off his shirt immediately.

Katharine nods her approval at his patience. "Good. Now, the shirt first, I think. Put it on the table behind you."

Steve tugs the shirt over his head in one swift move, then turns to deposit it as instructed. As he turns back around, Katharine has taken the few steps across the room toward him. She reaches a lazy finger out to touch his white tank top, plucking the shoulder strap between two fingers. She is so close he can smell her, her hair a hint of lavender, her skin a musk of vanilla, and he resists the urge to close his eyes and breathe her in.

"I haven't seen one of these since I lived at home with my father," she comments. "So old school." She takes a step to place herself squarely between his knees, placing both hands hard on his shoulders. "Too bad for you I don't have daddy issues," she says, fingers stroking quickly down his chest to tug the undershirt up and over his head. He feels it go with a slither of cotton against his skin, the feeling replaced by her hair as she quickly straddles him over the top of the chair. He can hear the stockings rubbing against his pants and wishes she would take those off so he can feel it against his skin. His hands reach out to caress her, to stroke those legs and that ass as she perches atop his hips.

"Oh no," she tells him in a decisive voice. "No touching for you. Not yet." She reaches behind him to retrieve something on the table behind him. "In fact," she says, "no looking either." He feels the blindfold as it hooks behind his ears and covers his surprised eyes, and then Steve sinks into a world of pure sensation. Katharine is still sitting on his lap, but he keeps his hands carefully at his sides, wanting to touch her but loving the feeling in his stomach that grows each second that he cannot.

She runs her hands down his face and around his neck, soft lips tracing fire around his collarbone as her hair brushes his nipples and causes the hair on his arms to stand erect.

His pants are incredibly tight, and he shifts his weight to relieve some of the pressure. "That must be so uncomfortable for you," she whispers against his skin, rubbing herself against his throbbing erection ever so slightly. Her hands trace light lines up his side, and he shivers, unable to stop himself from moving. He is smiling, a wide grin, and as her hands graze his skin, he giggles a little, the sensation a little too close to tickling.

Her hands stop at the sound, pressing hard and flat against his skin. "Oh no," she orders. "No sounds from you now. And certainly not any giggling." To punctuate her point, she arcs her fingers into little pinchers, tracing along his skin, pressing hard and then soft at intervals. Steve's face is turning red at the effort of restraint, his hands flexing uncontrollably at his sides.

"If you control it," she tells him, her breath warm on his skin, "you will be rewarded."

Her fingers skim down to the waist of his pants, pressing along the band and then sliding inside. He waits for the pause when she discovers the silky panties he wears, but if she is surprised, she doesn't show it with her hands.

"Naughty boy," she whispers, and her fingers begin their teasing again. He tenses, body

24

straining against her touch, wanting to laugh and trying desperately to keep it in, his cock hard against the satin confines of the panties. He moves a little on the seat, wanting to use his hands to adjust, but unwilling to disobey her order.

"Well done," she tells him when he restrains the urge to giggle once more. Her fingers work deftly at his waist, and then his pants are open. "Off," she says, standing up as she helps him move just enough to slip the pants off his hips. The khaki makes a lovely sound as it slides past the silky panties, and he represses another shiver. He knows it's not the forbidden giggle, but he wants to do all that she asks of him.

The pants slide down his legs, and then her hands are pulling them off, and he feels her kneel before him, her body warm against the inside of his legs. Her hands run teasing lines up and down his thighs, then inside his legs, and then up to where his cock waits, uncomfortably hard and tucked inside the restrictive panties.

"Oh, my," she says in a low voice. "You do have an issue there." Her hands move slowly, oh so slowly up the expanse of the panties, resting on the thin fabric that his shaft presses against. "Let's see," she comments, fingers moving delicately across the fabric, slipping it down with delicious slowness to release his throbbing erection. She doesn't remove the panties all the way, just pushes them down enough to let his cock free. The elastic band still presses hard against the base of his shaft, a reminder that he is not free, that she is in charge here. "Now," she says, and her tone is stern, "You will not make a sound. Understood?"

"Yes, Mistress."

Warmth engulfs his shaft, and he almost loses it right there, letting out a moan as he comes from the sensation. But somehow, he manages to hold on. She slides his cock in and out of her mouth slowly, delicately, not in any rhythm regular enough to bring him to the edge, and he's sure he will be able to do this, to please her, but then her hands start sliding up his side, fingers teasing and tickling, and the conflicting sensations are too much—the warm demands of her mouth and the deft pressure of her hands on his sensitive skin combining to test his limits, and he shudders, a giggle bursting free as he pulls away from her, a move he tries to control but cannot.

She retreats slowly but deliberately from his cock, tongue and lips leaving emptiness behind, and he pushes his hips up, trying to follow the sensation, but he can feel her pulling away, hands leaving his side as she stands up. He feels her leaning in before she speaks, her voice low and disappointed.

"Naughty boy," she tells him, and not in the sexy way she had commended his panties. "You didn't listen." At this, she lets out a sigh, and then her hands are sliding up his sides again, not tickling as before, but business-like and efficient. She reaches his shoulders, and then both hands slide up and pluck the blindfold from his eyes. "No coming for you today," she tells him, placing the blindfold on the table and taking a step away.

"Mistress, may I speak?" he begins, then waits for her to give permission.

"Go on," she says, face curious.

"I am sorry that I did not please you today. How can I make it up to you?"

She considers, cocking her head to the side as she stares at him. "Very well." She steps closer again, leaning forward so that her breasts are right in front of his face. Her hands reach down and pull the panties back up over his cock. "We will call this the One Week Challenge."

"And what is the challenge?" he asks. Katharine reaches behind him to grab his pants from the table, then hands them to him. As he stands and starts to put them on, she continues, "I want to see you again one week from tonight. Until then, you are not allowed to touch yourself."

Steve pauses with his hands on his zipper. "Define touching myself."

She steps forward again, her hand reaching out to cup his still hard cock. "This," she says, squeezing a little to emphasize what she means, "is mine. You may touch it as needed for the necessary parts of life, but you are not allowed to touch yourself for pleasure until I see you again."

"So no coming at all?"

"Absolutely no coming," she reiterates. "No touching that isn't required at all. This," she squeezes again, harder this time, and Steve's stomach does another one of those odd little excited flops, "is mine."

Steve nods, and she releases him.

"If you succeed, you will be rewarded," she grins, "but if you fail, there will be consequences," and the sweet grin turns wicked in a way that makes his heart pound in anticipation. It's almost enough to make him want to fail.

Almost.

Chapter Three

$\mathscr{T}$he first day is easy, and Steve wonders if this challenge will be as simple as it seems. But in bed that night, his phone pings. Steve doesn't have many friends, and certainly no one who would send him a message late at night. He picks it up and swipes the screen, cock already stiffening at the image of her face.

[KATHARINE: And how is my Naughty Boy doing so far?]

[STEVE: Very well, Mistress.]

Steve pauses, then bites his lip and types more.

[STEVE: Maybe this challenge is too easy, Mistress.]

There is a pause, and the phone buzzes again. This time there is no text, only a close-up of Katharine's tits, round and glorious with perky nipples. There is nothing identifiable in the picture, no hint of face or other body parts—just those amazing breasts in his face.

Steve's cock hardens immediately at the sight. A moment later, the phone buzzes again.

[KATHARINE: Still too easy for you?]

The picture of the breasts is still visible above her words, and Steve gets greedy.

[STEVE: Maybe a little bit, Mistress.]

He grins, a small thrill in his belly as he waits for her reply. He is not disappointed. A minute later, the phone buzzes again. This time, a hand is wrapped around one breast, fingers tipped with red nail polish squeezing the hard

nipple. Steve's cock jerks a little in his pants, and his hand slides down to touch himself. The phone buzzes before he can reach himself.

[KATHARINE: Remember the rules. No touching. That cock is MINE.]

Steve's hand drifts away from his hard cock, a slow ache growing in his balls. Maybe this week wouldn't be as easy as he thought.

Three days later, Steve is squirming on his bed, hands trapped beneath the small of his back, willing himself not to touch his hard dick. Katharine had sent two more pictures that night—one of her long leg encased in a black stocking, the other a close-up of her lips painted with fuck-me-red lipstick.

Five days later, Steve stands in the cold shower, trying not to see the words Katharine had sent that day.

You can do this, he tells himself, cock standing hard at attention despite the temperature of the water.

[KATHARINE: Imagine my mouth sucking on MY cock when I see you again. My tongue flicking the tip before I take it all the way inside to the back of my throat.]

That had almost undone him, but the next message sent him straight into the shower.

[KATHARINE: Imagine this silky pussy clenching around MY cock as I ride my way to pleasure. If you're lucky, I may bend you over before the end and have my way with that sweet asshole as well. I bet no one else has ever touched you there, not the way you want them to. Imagine how I will fuck that sweet ass until you beg for more.]

Standing in the shower, Steve lets the water run off his head and drip onto his hard cock. The image of her fucking him has him more excited than he expected. Of course, he's always excited by the thought of a girl riding his cock, but Katharine promising to peg him touches on desires he has barely begun to admit to himself.

I wonder what it will feel like, he muses, one hand trailing down first his hip and then sliding around to cup the round edge of his ass. Reaching just a little more, his finger brushes the edge of his asshole, and he shivers. His cock jerks. Steve takes his other hand and reaches down between his legs, avoiding his cock, but gripping his balls, sliding down just a little more to that sweet spot right between. Pleasure arcs through him.

I'm not touching my cock, he tells himself. *This is fine.*

Her cock, he reminds himself, both fingers pressing harder now. He imagines her lips, lipstick red like in the picture she sent, wrapping around his cock.

Still. Not. Touching. My...

The fantasy Katharine in his mind reaches out and tickles him mercilessly, never losing the rhythm of her mouth on his cock, and pleasure explodes over him. Cum sprays out into the shower, and Steve yanks his hands up, eyes widening.

Fuck.

Chapter Four

A week later, Steve stands in the hallway of Katharine's building, waiting until exactly 9pm to knock on her door. He bites his lip nervously, knowing that he will have to confess his crimes tonight. Excitement builds in his belly as he imagines the punishment she may inflict.

Maybe she'll beat me, he thinks, a small burn of hope in his chest.

Maybe she'll tease me again.

He pictures those delicious lips around his cock again, the warm heat of her making his cock stir to life despite himself. He tries to think of anything else, to calm down, but nothing helps. Any thought of Katharine only excites him more.

So when his watch shows 9:00, he knocks on her door with a raging hard-on. The door opens immediately, Katharine stepping aside to let him inside.

She wears a sexy teddy in green, the satin and lace complementing her skin and hair, though Steve can't stop staring at her tits plump and teasing him above the top of the low cups. She is barefoot this time, no stockings, and her hair is down, flowing over her shoulders and down her back.

"Take off your shoes," she orders, though her voice is softer than it can be, a strong suggestion rather than a command. Steve bends down to remove his shoes, abandoning them near the front door. "Take a seat," she tells him, gesturing to the same kitchen chair as last time. Steve obeys, quickly adjusting his cock through his pants as he sits.

Katharine walks slowly over to stand before him, her red toenails a perfect contrast against the hardwood floor. "So," she says, "how is my cock this evening?" She kneels before him, reaching up to stroke him through his pants. "Eager to get to it, I see." Unbuckling his belt, she bites her lip as she quickly undoes the button and lowers the zipper.

Steve waits for her response to his white lace panties, and he is rewarded with a big grin as she slides his pants down and off. "Nicely done," she praises him. "A good choice." She sits back on her haunches, those perfect breasts on display even with his lap. His cock strains against the lace.

"Now," she says, "how was my cock this week?"

Steve gulps, biting his lip as he looks down at her, knowing her tone will shift with his next words.

"Well..." he stalls.

Katharine leans back, face intense as she stares up at him. "Well what?" When he doesn't respond, Katharine sits up on her knees and slides his cock free of the panties. Her grip is hard, bordering on unpleasant. "What did you do with my cock this week, Naughty Boy?"

At her words, his cock hardens even more, and she narrows her eyes at him, hand scooting down to cradle his balls. "I thought we had an understanding," she tells him, gripping harder, pleasure spilling over into pain, but a small burst of joy explodes deep in his gut, and he holds back a smile.

"I am sorry, Mistress," he says.

Her hand tightens a little bit more, a burst of pain followed by that sweet joy. "Why are you sorry, Naughty Boy? What have you done with my cock?"

"I didn't touch it, Mistress!" he bursts, unable to stop himself. His cock jerks involuntarily in her grip, and she loosens a little bit.

"I believe you," she says, coaxing now. "So what did you touch?"

"Other parts," he whispers.

"Tell me," she demands. "Where did you touch yourself?"

Steve looks away from her demanding eyes, staring at the floor. "My ass," he admits, "and my balls."

"I see," Katharine purrs. "And what happened when you touched yourself?"

"I came," he confesses, gaze swinging back to meet hers, wanting to see her reaction.

"Do you remember the rules we established last week, Naughty Boy?" she asks, hand perfectly still on his cock. Steve longs for her to move against him, even if it is to squeeze him again. Any kind of sensation will do.

He nods. "I wasn't supposed to come," he says. "I wasn't supposed to touch myself."

Katharine smiles. "And you broke the rules," she tells him. "Now, what do you suppose should happen to naughty boys who break the rules?"

"They get beaten?" Steve asks, unable to stop the hopeful note that creeps into his voice. The image of her hands on his skin, or another implement smacking him, is arousing. The idea of being completely at her mercy is intoxicating.

Katharine smirks, no doubt knowing what he wants from her. "Maybe," she says, "but only obedient boys get beaten properly. Naughty boys need to be taught a lesson, so that the next time, they follow the rules."

"Yes, Mistress." Steve looks down at the floor, waiting for her punishment.

Katharine ponders for a moment, then releases his cock, sliding his panties up with business-like efficiency. "Stand up," she commands, getting to her feet. Steve obeys. "Take off your shirt," she tells him. Steve tugs his shirt and undershirt over his head, then stands there in his little pink panties, cock straining against the delicate lace, waiting for her next command. "Follow me," she orders, then heads deeper into the apartment, down a short hallway, and into a bedroom in the back corner.

A king-sized bed with a headboard perfect for bondage occupies most of the room, but instead of leading him to that, Katharine walks across the room to a dresser. She bends down, giving him a glorious view of her perfect ass in the g-string of the teddy, opens the bottom drawer, and pulls something out. Standing back up, she turns around, letting him see the device she holds. It is a metal contraption about the size of her palm with thick metal wires forged into a familiar shape.

"Do you know what this is?" she asks.

Steve nods. He's never seen a cock cage in person before, but he has the internet, and he's done his fair share of searches trying to scratch the itch deep inside. "Yes, Mistress."

"Have you used one before?" she continues.

Steve shakes his head. He's never been brave enough to try one before.

Katharine nods. "Good. This is perfect, then." She takes a few steps toward him, holding the device on the palm of her hand so he can see it more closely. "This part goes over your balls," she explains, finger circling the larger ring at the back, "and this is for my cock," he continues, running a finger along the curved cylinder of concentric circles. She flicks the small padlock on the front, twisting the key and opening the cage. "This key is mine, just like this cock is mine." She reaches out, sliding the panties down just enough to reveal his straining cock.

She sighs, shaking her head. "This will not do." She frowns, contemplating, then nods, struck by an idea. She hands him the cock cage along with the padlock and key. "Wait here."

She leaves him alone in the bedroom, and Steve examines the device. It will be restrictive, but it won't interfere with his ability to pee. He is glad that this cage doesn't include a sounding tip like some of the ones he has seen online. Maybe someday he will be ready to stick things inside his penis, but he's just not there yet.

He knows that he can't have a raging hard-on and put the cage on, and once on, it will make any erection he gets uncomfortable, bordering on painful, but the thought of wearing the cage and not having any way to remove it is exciting.

He will be at her complete mercy.

A shiver runs through him at the idea, and his cock jerks again. Steve hears Katharine's footsteps in the hallway behind him, but he doesn't turn to see her enter the room, staying exactly where he was as instructed.

When she reaches around him from behind, rubbing her breasts against his bare back, he is pleasantly surprised.

When she grabs his cock and cups his balls with a handful of ice, the shock goes through his entire body like an electric current. He stiffens, drops the cock cage, and then hunches over as the pain explodes through him. Katharine does not let go, moving with him as he huddles over himself, her grip merciless as the ice burns his sensitive skin.

Several agonizing moments pass before she releases him, and Steve sinks the rest of the way to the floor, kneeling first and then sliding onto his side, breath coming in shaking gasps. Katharine pushes on his hip, rolling him so he lays on his back on the cold floor, melted ice water dripping down between his ass cheeks to puddle on the floor beneath him. Most of the ice has melted, but her hands are still frigid when she grips him again, fitting the seemingly warm cock cage over his now limp penis. She grins wickedly as she snaps the padlock shut, then removes the key and slides it down the front of her teddy to nuzzle against her perfect breasts.

"Now," Katharine says, "perhaps this time you will follow the rules." She offers a hand to help Steve to his feet, and she leads him from the bedroom, down the hall, and back to where his pants and shirt still lay where he discarded them. She helps him dress, gentle but not inviting, even bending down to help with his shoes.

"So," she says when he is fully dressed and standing before her, "will you be a good boy this time for me?"

Steve nods, body still recovering from the shock. "Yes, Mistress," he manages, his voice unsteady.

"I have a long weekend coming up," Katharine says. "I expect you here on Friday night at 9pm, prepared to spend all three days with me."

"Yes, Mistress," Steve agrees.

"Until then, I will keep this key to my cock," she tells him. "There will be no playing with yourself—and there will be absolutely no coming until I allow it."

"Yes, Mistress," Steve says, that small burn in his belly back again at the idea of the next 48 hours spent at her mercy.

He can hardly wait.

Chapter Five

*T*wo nights later, Steve paces in the hallway outside of Katharine's door. He adjusts himself, glad that despite the discomfort of the last two days, he still managed to wear a pair of green silky panties.

He hasn't touched himself except for the bare minimum, and while the idea of the cock cage is exciting, and knowing that he cannot free himself is thrilling, two days is a very long time to be restrained, and Steve is ready for his punishment to be over.

He knocks at precisely the hour as instructed, and Katharine lets him in immediately. Steve only takes a brief moment to appreciate her outfit, the dark blue satin robe hugging her curves and ending at the apex of her thighs. She leads him to the familiar kitchen chair and directs him to sit.

"And how is my Naughty Boy tonight?" she purrs. "Have you learned your lesson?"

"Oh yes, Mistress," Steve says, squirming on the chair. He hasn't been able to sit for very long, his sensitive skin nearly raw in some places from the metal rings. It hasn't been too painful beyond the morning wood he couldn't avoid, but the morning's erection lasted longer than he wanted, encouraged by thoughts of Katharine, and the metal rings dug in certain places. Luckily, his job allows him to work from home, and he can do most of what he needs at his convertible standing desk. He never thought he'd need to elevate the desk because of a cock cage, but he's not sorry for the experience.

Though he is ready for it to be over.

Katharine leans down, hands reaching for his belt and slowly, gently unbuttoning his pants. "Let's see my poor battered cock," she coos. "I'm so proud of you!" she exclaims at the sight of his green panties. "These are lovely!"

Steve smiles, that low thrill back in his belly at the idea of pleasing her. "Thank you, Mistress," he says quietly.

"Oh you poor thing," she says, sliding down the panties to reveal his cock jammed against the rings of the cage. She meets his eyes. "Will you follow the rules in the future?" she asks, a command in the words.

Steve nods. "Oh yes, Mistress. What do you want me to do?"

Katharine purses her lips, contemplating. Finally, she nods, then reaches into a small pocket in her robe and retrieves the key. A quick flick of her fingers, and the cage is removed, his cock free, and Steve sighs at the new ache that spreads from his balls. "There you go," she says, setting the cage on the table behind him. She sits back on her haunches, then stands up, holding out a hand to help him stand.

Steve obeys, the bottom of his shirt brushing against his tender cock, and a shiver runs through him. Katharine reaches out and slides both shirts over his head, pressing her breasts against his chest as she does so, the motion of his shirt replaced by the satiny feel of her robe against his skin. Steve takes a deep breath, trying to calm himself, not wanting to disappoint her again.

"Come with me," she says, then takes his hand and leads him down the hallway to the back bedroom. Instead of making him stand in the middle of the floor like last time, though, she leads him through another door into a master bathroom. She lets go of his hand when she walks over to the huge walk-in shower, opening the glass door and leaning in to turn on the water. Her robe scoots up a little, revealing the glorious bottom of her ass cheeks, and Steve hardens a little bit, the feeling quickly followed by another ache.

Standing up, Katharine smiles at him, then reaches for the tie at her waist. She removes it, then lets the robe fall open, revealing a body that Steve has only fantasized about. Perfect breasts, a flat stomach, a waxed pussy, and those long luscious legs. She lets the robe slide down her shoulders slowly, abandoning it when it falls to the floor around her feet.

"Come in," she says, reaching out her hand to him again. "Let me see to my obedient boy."

Steve takes her head and lets her lead him into the shower. The water is warm, pulsing from several rainshower jets in the ceiling, the kind of shower Steve has only seen in porn. There is a small bench at the back of the large space, but the shower stall is big enough for him to lie down easily. Katharine pulls Steve to the center of the shower, then begins to lather him in soap and scrub him gently with a loofah sponge. The water stings his raw skin at first, but then Steve forgets about it as other sensations overwhelm his senses: Katharine's warm, wet skin sliding across his as she washes his back, her fingernails against his scalp as she washes his hair, the gentle press of her hands as she washes his cock and balls.

"Don't come," she orders. She rinses him, then takes him gently in her mouth, the feeling of her warmth only slightly cooler than the hot water. She sucks him slowly, easily, teasing his length as she kneels before him, eyes closed as the water runs down her body.

Steve tries to calm down, to think of other things, but it's too much, and he grabs her head, pulling himself out of her mouth just before he comes. "I—" he manages, gasping. "I can't—" He looks down at her disappointed face. "Mistress, I..."

Katharine sighs, getting to her feet. "And here I thought you understood the rules."

"I do, Mistress. You're just so good at that. I can't help myself."

"Good at what, Naughty Boy?" she asks, standing up and pressing a hand to the center of his chest.

"Good at sucking cock, Mistress," Steve replies, stepping slowly as she continues to press him back. "You are so beautiful," he whispers to the goddess pushing him to the bench.

"Sit," she commands, and he obeys, sitting on the edge of the bench, his face even with her breasts. She frowns, no doubt thinking of what to do with him, then she smiles at him. "You think I'm beautiful, Naughty Boy?"

Steve nods. "Oh yes, Mistress. So fucking perfect. My goddess."

Katharine raises an eyebrow. "Goddess?" she echoes. "Then show me how you worship your goddess, Steve."

"May I touch you, Mistress?"

Katharine nods.

"Fuck yes," Steve moans, leaning forward to suck her nipple, using one hand to fondle the other one while his other hand slides down the curve of her waist to cup her hip. He sucks hard, then nibbles gently, looking up to see her reaction.

Katharine smiles, pleased. Steve grins, moving his mouth to her other nipple as he slides both hands down to rest on her hips. He releases her nipple to look down at the smooth skin of her pussy. He slides off the bench to his knees, hands drifting down to caress her thighs. He looks up at her, water running down his face, but he blinks through it. "May I lick your pussy, Mistress?" he asks, fingers hovering just outside the perfect spot between her legs.

Katharine nods, a wry grin crossing her lips. "You may try. But naughty boys often don't know how to do a proper job of it," she tells him.

"I will try," Steve agrees, then leans in, using his hands to separate her legs a little bit so he has room to work. Steve may not be a perfect lover, but there are certain skills he excels at, and licking pussy is one of them, drilled into him by his first lover, a woman who demanded several oral orgasms before she would even think about letting him put his cock inside of her. Steve didn't mind. He enjoys the sounds that women make when he finds the perfect spot, the exact rhythm.

Steve moves slowly, licking her skin in lazy strokes while he eases his fingers lower to run the outside of her opening. Katharine stiffens, and when Steve looks up, he sees that she is watching him carefully, eyes calculating. He rubs the outside of her opening again, sliding his thumbs gently against the sensitive skin, and her legs tighten—a good sign. Steve leans forward, mouth going to work immediately, licking her clit with careful strokes, noting when her legs stiffen and when she relaxes. When he figures out the spots she prefers and the rhythm she wants, he wraps one arm around her, cupping her ass and holding her close. His other hand continues to rub slowly, fingers slipping in and out of her in matching rhythm to his tongue.

Katharine moans, her hands reaching down to twist in his hair, and Steve continues to lick in the same rhythm, knowing that she is close now. He adds another finger inside her, and she tightens immediately, hips shuddering as he continues to lick her clit.

"Oh fuck!" she cries, hands latching onto his head as her body shakes in his arms. Steve tightens the arms around her back, supporting her weight as her legs turn rubbery, continuing to nuzzle her clit until she tells him to stop. "That was well done," she says when she catches her breath, looking down at him between her legs. "Exceptionally well done," she admits.

"May I lick your pussy some more, Mistress?" Steve asks. "It's so delicious. I just want to lick you all night long."

Katharine preens, enjoying his words, but she shakes her head. "I don't think I can stand for another orgasm like that," she admits. "My legs are jello."

"Then sit on my face," Steve suggests, swiveling his body so he sits on his butt, then scooting down so he lays on his back on the floor between her legs. "Let me eat that pussy some more, Mistress," he begs. "I need you on my face."

"I'll be the one needing things," she orders, but she kneels over him, moving up so her legs are on either side of his face. Slowly, she lowers herself until her body touches his lips. Steve gives her a moment to get situated, her hands resting on the bench behind him, then reaches both hands up to grip her ass. This is his favorite position. He grips her tightly, refusing to let her move, then attacks her clit again, the same steady strokes he now knows she likes while one hand slips below his chin and into her again, pressing up and forward to stroke her g-spot. Katharine moans, hips rocking, but his arm holds her steady. He breathes through his nose, loving the spectacle above him, Katharine's perfect breasts jutting out, her hair a riot of darkness and water as she tilts her head back and forth in her pleasure.

"Fucking yes!" she yells, and then she is shuddering again, thighs thrumming against his face as the orgasm rips through her. "You are quite talented for a Naughty Boy!"

"Again, Mistress?" he begs, but Katharine is already pulling away, sliding down to sit on his chest before she leans forward and kisses him hard, tongue eager in his mouth, tracing the line of his teeth.

"I'm going to fuck you, Naughty Boy," she tells him, sucking on his lips. "You deserve it after that performance."

"Thank you Mistress," Steve says, watching as she slides that glorious body farther down, settling herself above the hard rod of his cock.

"You are not allowed to come," she orders, then slams down with a jerk of her hips, engulfing him completely.

Steve's eyes close as the intensity of her pussy around his cock overwhelms him, and then open again. He wants to watch her ride him, wants to see those perfect titties bounce and jerk as she moves faster.

"That's good," she groans, leaning back as she lifts herself up and then back down on him, pressing him deep inside. "That's so fucking good!"

"Can I touch you, Mistress?" Steve asks, hands fisted at his side as he longs to caress those tits.

"You may," she allows, moving again.

Instead of reaching to cup her breasts as he desires, Steve moves his hands to press against her clit again, using one to grip her round ass as the other rubs a small circle over her clit. Katharine looks down at his hand and then his face, a wide smile on her face. "You are good!" she exclaims. Steve continues to rub, watching her breasts but also focusing on his hands because he knows if he spends too much time watching her tits bounce in front of his face, he's going to lose it and come. If he tries to grip them, it will all be over.

Instead, he concentrates on making Katharine come again, this time on his cock, and the grip of her pussy almost sends him over the edge, but he manages to pull back at the last moment, both hands on her hips holding her steady under the guise of supporting her after her orgasm.

Katahrine catches her breath, then leans down to kiss him again, the water rushing over them both. "Very nice," she tells him. "I may even let you lick my pussy again."

"Thank you, Mistress," Steve says, looking up at the gorgeous woman still atop him.

It's going to be a long weekend, and he's looking forward to every moment.

Chapter Six

*S*teve stands in the center of Katharine's bedroom, staring at himself in the full length mirror on her closet door. He wears a classic French maid outfit: black dress with a white apron, black ribbon tied around his neck, white thigh high stockings connected to black garters, and a pair of sensible low heels that he can actually walk around in.

Steve doesn't ask how Katharine has the outfit in his size, especially the shoes. He wants to assume she ordered it for him; she spent enough time undressing him over the last few weeks, enough time for her to see his sizes and order it. Though the idea that she has other men in her house, completing the same tasks, is both intimidating and exciting.

He is officially Katharine's Naughty Boy now.

Steve adjusts the small white cap on his head, smirking at his reflection. He's never thought about fully crossdressing before, but he finds he enjoys the experience, especially the padded bra wrapped over his shoulders and clipped behind his back. It took a few tries to figure out the motion, but Katharine helped him. Looking at his reflection, Steve decides that when this is over, he might order some more clothing of his own and explore his options.

But for now, he's going to enjoy every moment of this weekend.

Nodding at himself, he heads into the living room, finding Katharine resting on the couch, feet propped beneath her as she leans on the arm of the couch, book open on her lap.

"Mistress?" he asks quietly.

"You can start in the kitchen," she says, gesturing to the galley kitchen behind him.

Steve nods, then heads into the kitchen, enjoying the tap of the heels as they echo on the wooden floor. He wipes down the counters first, tidying items and putting everything in the cabinets where he finds similar items. The dishes are easy enough: a single plate, silverware, a glass cup, and one small pan.

While he works his way through her refrigerator, cleaning the shelves and organizing her food, he heats up a pot of water on the stove, delivering his mistress a hot cup of tea, along with several tea cookies, on a small tray. She smiles her approval at the gesture, then nods to the small door in the hallway. Steve opens it to find a broom and mop snapped into a rack on the inside of the door, a bucket on the floor, and shelves of messily jammed towels and sheets.

Steve rolls his shoulders, gearing up for his next task, then empties the entire contents of the closet onto the kitchen table. He folds the towels into the exact same size, piling them according to color, then fights the sheets and blankets into similar submission, tidying her closet with the same efficiency that he used in her kitchen. Seeing the finished product excites him a little, but not as much as her nod of approval at the sight.

He continues his cleaning, sweeping her entire house and then mopping the kitchen and living room, gently lifting her feet back onto the couch when he moves beneath her. While the floor dries, he moves into the bathroom, scrubbing the shower and tub until they shine. He doesn't know Katharine has appeared behind him until something smacks his bare ass while he is on his knees cleaning the toilet. His body jerks, cock hardening instantly at the impact, and he pauses, eagerly waiting for the next blow.

It doesn't come.

After a long moment, Steve looks over his shoulder to see Katharine standing behind him holding a small plastic ruler. She nods at the toilet, and Steve turns back to his work.

A moment later, another smack lands across his ass, and he jerks forward, cock pressing against the cold porcelain for a brief second before he pulls back—right into another smack. Steve redoubles his efforts, wanting to finish cleaning and stand up before he loses control and comes all over the clean floor. Katharine watches him work, but she doesn't smack him again.

When he finishes the bathroom, she leads him toward the bedroom, opening three dresser drawers to reveal a trove of sex toys. She hands him the spray cleaner and a roll of paper towels, then sets herself up on the bed, watching him as she lazily flips through a magazine. Steve grins, cock hard but not on the edge of exploding, then sets to work. He lays out each item on the top of the dresser, working through one drawer at a time. There is an array of dildos in different shapes and sizes: some that vibrate, some with wide suction cup bases, some of glass and metal. The prostate massagers are next, a series from small to obnoxiously large.

When Steve finishes those, Katharine gets off the bed and approaches him. "Kneel on the floor," she tells him, "and lay your chest on the bed." Her bed is low to the ground, so Steve obeys easily, his ass exposed as the maid outfit rides up his waist. The stockings tug against his thighs as the garters pull tight, a pressure he enjoys. He hears Katharine move over the dresser and then the sound of her picking something up off the top—an item he just cleaned then.

She approaches him from behind, sinking to her knees and sliding up to press her body against his skin. He enjoys the slide of her silk robe against his ass, but then her hands are sliding toward his cock, enfolding him gently and stroking ever so slowly. Her other hand finds his ass, and her fingers massage him, easing around the edge. Steve shudders at the combination of sensations, straining back against her, wanting more.

Her hands abandon him for a moment, and he hears the sound of a bottle being opened, then warm wet hands grasp his cock and rub his asshole at the same time. Katharine is gentle, careful to keep a slow rhythm on his cock with one hand as she presses her other thumb inside of him. When he eases, her thumb vanishes, replaced by something slightly larger, one of the prostate massagers he laid on top of the counter. Steve imagines the shape as it slowly fills his ass, small at first, then gradually larger until it reaches an apex and immediately shrinks again before the wide base. He tightens as the dildo presses deeper, and Katharine waits until he relaxes again, hand caressing his cock gently, pleasure building as he explores the new sensations. By the time she gets the entire dildo in his ass, Steve's cock is weeping, and Katharine is gentle as she tugs a stretchy rubber ring around his balls, securing the dildo in place.

"Stand up," she says quietly, backing away and letting Steve find his feet. The dildo in his ass is a new feeling, and he moves slowly, enjoying the pleasure as it hits different places inside of him. When he is back on his feet and fairly steady, Katharine smiles and gestures back to the dresser. "Continue," she says, leaving the room. Steve hears the water turn on the bathroom, presumably Katharine washing her hands.

He works his way through the rest of the drawers, unearthing a wide array of treasures: anal beads, leather whips, rubber flogs, a trove of buzzy bullets, and more restraints types than Steve imagined existed.

He hears Katharine re-enter the room just as he is finishing up. "Mistress, may I ask a question?"

Katharine nods. "Sure."

"Where did you get all of this stuff? The internet?"

Katharine smirks. "Fetish Circuit," she replies.

Steve cocks his head, nearly losing his little cap. He reaches up to straighten it. "What's that?" he asks.

"Continue to please me, Naughty Boy," Katharine purrs, "and I will show you."

"Thank you, Mistress," Steve says. "What next?" He is willing to do more work, but the dildo in his ass has him rock hard, and he will struggle not to come if she makes him do much more.

"I think you've paid enough attention to my home," she says, biting her lip. "I think it's time you paid some attention to me."

"Please, Mistress," Steve says. "What would you like? A massage? I can rub away all of your stress. Or your feet?" Steve glances at her bare feet. "Can I paint your toenails, Mistress? Rub your feet and suck your toes?"

Katharine laughs, then sits down on the bed with a shrug. "Sure. The nail polish is in the bathroom cabinet."

"What color?" Steve asks.

"Surprise me," Katharine replies, lying down so her robe reveals all of her gorgeous legs.

"Yes, Mistress," Steve replies, heading to the bathroom. He returns with more supplies than a bottle of nail polish, carrying a small tub filled with warm bubbly water and a towel, leaving once to collect a small bottle of massage oil.

Steve lifts her legs, gently placing her feet in the tub of water, removing one and rubbing it. He takes his time, sucking each toe as he promised. Katharine doesn't seem to enjoy it more than anything else, but Steve's cock weeps again as her delicate toes fill his mouth, loving the notion of literally licking his goddess's feet.

He is in the middle of sucking the toes on her other foot when she reaches a hand into the small pocket of her robe, and squeezes something inside. The dildo inside Steve's ass purrs to life, vibrations flooding through him.

Steve spits out her toe with a gasp, entire body electrified, and then Katharine squeezes again, and the sensation ceases, leaving Steve shuddering. It is too much—he explodes into an orgasm, cum coating the inside of the maid's outfit.

"Did you just come, you Naughty Boy?" Katharine asks, removing her hand to show him a small black remote control.

"I'm sorry, Mistress," Steve gasps, still unable to say more.

Katharine frowns, then pushes the button again. The dildo vibrates again, this time stimulating incredibly sensitive flesh, and Steve hunches into himself, the pleasure too much to bear. Finally, Katharine stops. Steve spends a few moments catching his breath.

"I didn't know it would do that, Mistress," Steve says. "Please forgive me."

"Hmm," Katharine continues to frown. "You've been so good today. I wanted to reward you. Now you have to earn your way back into my graces." She gives him a stern look. "No more coming without permission," she orders. "Now I have to think about a punishment."

Steve nods, returning to her feet with double the attention as she ponders. When he paints her toenails, his execution is perfect, every line precise and not a single mark on her skin. He moves to her legs next, rubbing her with oil and easing the tension from her calves with strong hands. He pauses when she leans up.

"Move your leg over here," she demands. Steve leans back, swinging his lower body around so one stockinged leg rests on the bed next to her. She frowns at the low-heeled shoe on her blanket, and takes it off, chucking it aside to land on the floor. Her hands move quickly up his leg, efficient rather than sexy, seeking the hooks of the garter belt. She releases the top of the stocking, and it snaps down his leg, revealing a hairy thigh and large kneecap. Katharine nods, lifting a small group of hairs up and away from his skin with two fingers before releasing them to curl back against his thigh. "Take them off," she gestures at the stockings.

Steve stands up, fumbling with the hooks before letting the other stocking slide down. He is relieved to release the pressure around his thighs, but sorry to lose the silky feel of the stockings against his skin. He slides both down slowly, relishing the feel before tugging them off his feet.

"Now," she says, sitting up, "go to the bathroom, and bring back hot water in this tub, a towel, shaving cream, and the razor in the cabinet."

Steve's eyes widen as he realizes what she means to do. He has always fantasized about shaving a woman's legs, but he has never thought about shaving his own. He obeys, returning with the items. Katharine has him sit on the bed, then spreads the towel out beneath his legs.

A small grin crosses her lips as she looks up at his face. "Have you ever done this before?"

Steve shakes his head. "I've shaved my face," he says. "But that's it."

"So you should pay attention," Katharine suggests, and Steve nods.

She begins slowly, gently, dipping her hands in the warm water and running them over his legs to get them wet, then running a line of cream down one leg. She massages the cream, smearing the foam from his ankle to his thigh, and Steve pulls the dress out of the way to rest on his belly, exposing the crinoline. She takes the razor and makes a smooth line up his shin, the hair and shaving cream gathering on the razor to leave a mostly smooth swath of skin beneath. She rinses the razor in the water and repeats the motion, shaving his legs in delicate strips. She does an entire pass, then re-lathers him in foam and repeats the process, catching the stray hairs that still linger. Steve watches with a mix of erotic and clinical interest, learning the technique while soaking in the sensations.

When he has one smooth leg and one hairy leg, she hands him the razor. She lathers his leg, then guides his hand as he removes his hair, pressing harder here, and easier there. When he finishes, she gestures for him to stay where he is. She gathers the tub and heads into the bathroom; Steve hears the water running as she empties the dirty water. She returns with a small bottle of lotion, and slowly rubs down his legs, the cream soothing the irritated parts of his skin. Then, she takes his hand and runs it down the newly shaven skin. Steve shivers at the sensation, then looks at her.

"Mistress," he says meekly, hands on his thighs, "May I ask a question?"

"What is it?" Katharine replies, head cocked to one side as she considers their work.

"May I shave your legs?" he asks, the fantasy finally a possibility. "I would be so honored."

"Are you saying my legs are hairy?" she asks.

"Of course not, Mistress," he says, not wanting to upset her. He's not lying. She has the very beginning of stubble. He wouldn't have noticed if he didn't have a long-standing desire to shave a woman's legs.

Katharine sits back, pursing her lips. "You really want to shave my legs?"

"Please?" Steve asks, knowing there is a pleading note in his voice that he can't hide.

Katharine shrugs, flopping down on the bed. "Sure," she tells him with a shrug. "Let;s see what you've learned."

"Oh thank you Mistress!" Steve practically leaps off the bed, returning a few minutes later with more supplies: a clean towel and a fresh tub of warm water.

"Are you ready, Mistress?"

Katharine is smiling, and she lets him watch as she reaches for the remote again, pressing the button and enjoying his expression as the vibrations tingle through him again. She turns it off after a moment, careful not to let him get too close again.

"I thought I should do that now, before you have a razor in your hand."

"Very wise, Mistress."

Steve doesn't speak as he works, spreading the shaving cream with soft strokes, rinsing the razor in the warm water after he runs it over the lines of her skin. He spends time rubbing the massage oil into her skin after he finishes, careful to moisturize those luscious legs.

His cock is hard again by the time he finishes and begins setting items aside. He puts everything away, then returns to find her still lying on the bed where he left her, face close to dozing.

"I think I may nap," she says. "That was so perfectly relaxing."

"Very well, Mistress," Steve says. "I will continue to clean."

Katharine nods, and Steve leaves her in the bed, returning to his tasks, enjoying the thrill of the dildo as he continues to please his mistress. The buzzing of the dildo tells him that she is awake again, and he returns to the bedroom to find her blinking lazily at him.

"You've been so good today. Mostly," she says. "You know what else a good maid does, my boy?" Katharine asks, sliding her robe up to reveal her smooth pussy.

"What's that, Mistress?" Steve asks, sitting down on the edge of the bed.

"He makes sure the mistress is completely satisfied in every way."

Steve nods, adjusting himself beneath the maid outfit, not wanting to embarrass himself again. "What would satisfy the Mistress?" he asks, moving closer.

Katharine's robe has slid up to puddle across her belly. As he watches, she tugs the sides apart, revealing those glorious breasts. Steve's cock hardens again, pressing awkwardly against the tulle underneath the maid's uniform. "I am here to serve," he breathes, shifting a little to move his cock away from the scratchy crinoline.

"Then I think you should lick this pussy, Steve," she orders, casually reaching over to the small pile of work material on the night table. She ignores the closed laptop, the file folders, instead plucking a familiar plastic ruler from the top of the pile and leaning up on her elbows. She gestures with the ruler. "I know how well you lick pussy, Steve. Let's see how well you can follow orders."

Chapter Seven

Steve tugs her closer to the edge of the bed, kneeling on the floor and settling himself between her thighs. He wants to be comfortable for a long while, but the dildo in his ass makes other positions too tantalizing, and he knows if he lays down, his cock rubbing against the bed as he moves will bring him too close to the edge.

He slides both hands under her thighs and moves her pussy closer, leaning down to breathe in her scent. He starts slowly, softly, with gentle kisses down her lips, fingers teasing her opening, allowing her to open to him, rocking her hips to give him better access.

"That's quite lovely," she moans, and Steve is rewarded by the joy of the dildo buzzing to life in his ass. He struggles to keep his current pace, fingers deftly circling the outer edge of her lips while his tongue moves ever closer to her clit. The dildo stops, and Steve is able to focus again.

"Suck my clit," she demands a moment later, and Steve obeys, nuzzling her clit with his tongue while sucking. "And finger me!" she adds. Steve's finger slides inside, marveling at her wetness, the way her pussy tightens on his fingers, imagining that his cock is inside her instead.

His dick jerks at the idea, and a few seconds later, the dildo vibrates again, his reward to following her instructions perfectly. Steve allows himself to enjoy the feeling, mouth working hard against her body, fingers sliding in and out, feeling her response and adjusting to her needs, and soon, her thighs tighten, pressing hard against his cheeks. Steve keeps the same rhythm, knowing that she needs him to focus in order to come. She shudders, pussy locking onto his fingers.

"Fuck yes!" she yells, a hand burying itself in his hair, knocking the white cap aside. "You are so good at that!" She gasps, then leans back. A second later, the vibration stops as she remembers the remote. "Sorry," she says. "I shouldn't have left that on so long."

"I am fine, Mistress," Steve says. "There's nowhere else I'd rather be than here, worshiping your pussy."

"Make me come again," she demands, whacking the top of his head with the ruler, "and I just may let you come tonight."

Steve bends his head down, mouth sucking her clit as his fingers slide back inside. He knows her body now, knows what she likes, and within minutes, she is on the edge again, the ruler thumping against his head as she urges him on.

"Oh, like that," she moans, "please keep doing that!" In her ecstacy, she has forgotten her role as Mistress, begging him for release. Steve chuckles, fingers moving in rhythm with his mouth, and then both her hands are wrapped in his hair, pressing him against her as her entire body shakes and shivers.

"Fuck yes!" she screams, shuddering against his face. Steve retreats, hands pulling out of her and cupping her ass as he rests his cheek on her thigh, waiting for her to regain her senses.

When Katharine's breathing regulates, she leans up to look down at him. "Naughty Boy," she says, "I think I may have to keep you."

"I'd like that, Mistress," Steve says, placing a kiss on her thigh.

"Will you follow the rules?" she asks.

"I will try," he says, knowing the hint of resistance will please her. She enjoys punishing him when he breaks the rules.

And he loves being punished.

"Very well," she says, sitting up all the way. She runs her hands through his hair, straightening the mess she made, then gently moves him off her thigh, standing up and walking over to the closet. Steve sinks to the side, sitting on the floor, the dildo pressing into him with delicious new friction.

Steve watches her walk, that glorious body flushed from orgasms and lovely as she opens the door. He's a bit curious to see the inside. Judging by the rest of her apartment, he expects a jumble of clothing. Instead, he is rewarded by a clean line of color coded dresses next to perfectly sorted shirts and skirts. Two rows of shoes line the floor, from sandals to thigh high boots folded over. She reaches for a small set of drawers in the center of the closet and removes an item. Steve sees that there are other similar items in the drawer, and he looks back at the perfectly organized clothes.

How many Naught Boys does she have? The idea that others have cleaned her house sparks both jealousy and joy. Steve doesn't want to be her one and only, doesn't want any of the normal relationship crap from her. He just wants to worship her, to please her, to be among those worthy enough to lick her pussy.

And the thought that another man, a stronger man, fucks her before he does starts a small fire in his belly that promises to devour him.

I want to watch, he decides. *At least once, I want to watch her with another man, and I want to lick the cum from her pussy.*

A slow smile crosses his face at the image, and when Katharine walks back over to him, she returns the smile. She holds a black leather collar in her hand, a thin band with a metal buckle and a silver loop that she can hook things to.

"Will you be collared by me?" she asks.

Steve nods, mouth suddenly dry. "Yes, Mistress."

"Come here then." She gestures to the floor in front of her.

Steve rocks onto his knees, crawling over to her. When he reaches her feet, he licks her toes, then sits back on his haunches. Katharine smiles, then unties the thin black ribbon tied around his neck. She drops it on the floor.

The leather is cool against his skin and tight when she buckles it. "You will wear this when you are with me," she tells him. "This shows me that you are my Naughty Boy."

"Yes, Mistress," Steve agrees, swallowing and feeling the restriction of the leather against his neck.

Katharine turns around, returning to the closet for one more item. Steve admires the curve of her ass as she turns.

She returns with another strip of leather, this one much smaller and more ordinary. She gestures for Steve's wrist and he lifts it up, letting her slide the leather bracelet around his wrist and tightening it against his skin. "You will wear this at all times. It's my mark on you," she says.

"Yes, Mistress," Steve says. "Thank you, Mistress."

"Now," she says, lifting him to his feet. Steve bobs on his feet for a second, readjusting to the low heels. The back of his feet will have blisters tomorrow, but he doesn't care.

"Yes, Mistress?" Steve asks, looking down at her from his full height, enhanced now by the shoes.

"Kiss me," she orders.

Steve bends down, meeting her lips with a soft kiss that quickly turns passionate. He has licked other parts of her body, had her mouth around his cock and her fingers in his ass, but he has never kissed her like this before, and the sensation is intoxicating. Their shower kisses were frantic but quick; this is long and filled with promise. His arms reach around her body, one hand cupping her ass and the other reaching around to squeeze one perfect titty. His cock jerks, hard against her belly, and her hands slide up his arms and around his neck, twisting in his hair as she explores his mouth.

"Undress," she whispers against his mouth. "I want to see you."

Steve lifts the dress over his head in one motion, eager to free his cock from the rough, and slightly crusty, crinoline beneath, then reaches around awkwardly to remove the bra. Katharine kneels before him as he steps out of the shoes, unhooking the garter and sliding each stocking down his legs. She leaves the dildo in place, hands carefully avoiding his cock as she undresses him. When he stands before her wearing only the collar, she stands up and grabs his hair in a fist.

"Now," she breathes against his mouth, gripping his hair painfully as she holds him in place, "I want you to fuck me, Naughty Boy. Fuck me hard. And well." She tugs on his head, looking at him intensely. "Fuck me well, Boy, and you will be allowed to come."

"Yes, Mistress," Steve says. He reaches out to cup her ass and lifts her. Katharine wraps her legs around his waist, taking some of the weight off his arms. Steve isn't a big guy, and he's not super strong, but Katharine is small, and he can carry her for a little while like this. The feel of her naked body rubbing against his is plenty of motivation to hold her tight.

Instead of taking her to the bed, as he imagines she expects him to, he walks over to the wall instead, resting her back against the wall exactly across the room from the full-length mirror he admired himself in earlier.

"Watch me fuck you, Mistress," he says, adjusting himself to line up his cock, then remembers he is her submissive. "Will you watch me fuck you?"

Katharine gasps, the idea delighting her as her gaze slips from his face to look over his shoulder, seeing herself pinned against the wall by his body. "Yes, Naughty Boy," she says. "Now fuck me well!"

Steve doesn't wait for more encouragement, pushing his cock inside of her in one hard thrust. Katharine moans, her pussy warm and soaking wet around his cock, and Steve pulls back and plunges in again. Katharine's eyes close as her head tilts back, completely lost in the sensation, and Steve reverts to his old bedroom habits, fucking her hard and fast, enjoying the thud of her back against the wall, the slapping wet sound of his body pounding into hers, the glassy eyed pleasure on her face.

The dildo in his ass intensifies every motion, but Steve holds himself back. He's on familiar territory here, and he knows how to wait to come, though the dildo adds another layer of pleasure to each stroke.

"How is that, Mistress?" he asks, but the words are more of a demand than a request, and then Katharine is shuddering on his cock, pussy gripping him hard as she comes. "You like coming on your cock?"

"So...good..." she moans, body going limp for a second.

Steve pauses, waiting for her to come back, cock buried deep inside of her. She has bitten his shoulder, the pain a dull thud only registering now that he has paused, but the mark will remain for several days. Steve wants more like them.

"May I continue, Mistress?" he asks, voice more submissive again.

"Please," she whispers. "I want more." Steve moves slowly at first, easing her back into the rhythm, and then she is gripping his shoulders hard, eyes skipping between the picture of them in the mirror behind him and the collar around his neck. When she is close again, she reaches up to grab his hair, looking deep into his eyes.

"Come for me, Naughty Boy," she orders. "I need you to come for me!"

Steve bends down, claiming her mouth with a painfully hard, bruising kiss, biting her lips and scorching her tongue as he pounds her against the wall, finally allowing himself to let go.

The orgasm screams through him, and Katharine yells out her release as they come together. He pumps a few more times, body still shuddering around the dildo, overwhelmed by the warm heat of her pussy, and then they both slowly slide down the wall to land in a crumpled heap on the floor. Steve ends up on his back on the floor, Katharine's body wrapped around him. For a few long moments, neither speaks, each regaining breath and slowing pounding heartbeats.

Finally, Katharine sits up, the movement of her pussy pushing his cock out of her. She immediately reaches for it, adjusting her body so his soft dick presses against her again.

"Oh no," she groans, looking down at him, still breathing heavily on the floor. "That won't do." She reaches around, clearly searching for something on the floor.

The dildo in Steve's ass roars to life, and his cock jerks, hardening again as she finds the remote control.

"That's much better," she says, pushing his semi-erect cock back inside of her. "I expect my Naughty Boy to come at least two more times tonight."

Steve smiles up at her. "Yes, Mistress. As you wish."

Ali Whippe

*A*li Whippe is the pen name of a professor in the higher education system who delights in imagining naughty distractions while enduring endless mind-numbing committee meetings. She loves to push the boundaries of the written word and the imagination, knowing that life at work would be way more exciting if more people didn't wear panties.

More Books by Ali Whippe
Office Hours
Tutoring Center
Athletics
Extra Credit
Bound for Release
Fetish Circuit

Beau and Professor Bestialora
The Goat's Gruff
Goldie and Her Three Beards
Pied Piper's Pipe
Princess Pea's Bed

LGBT Erotica

GRAYSON ACE
How I Got Here
First Year Out of the Closet
You're Only a Top?
You're Only a Bottom?
I Think I'm a Serial Swiper

LEO SPARX
Claiming Alexander
Taming Alexander
Saving Alexander

4HorsemenPublications.com

www.ingramcontent.com/pod-product-compliance
Lightning Source LLC
Chambersburg PA
CBHW030213130726
47898CB00012B/1004